The Great Quillow

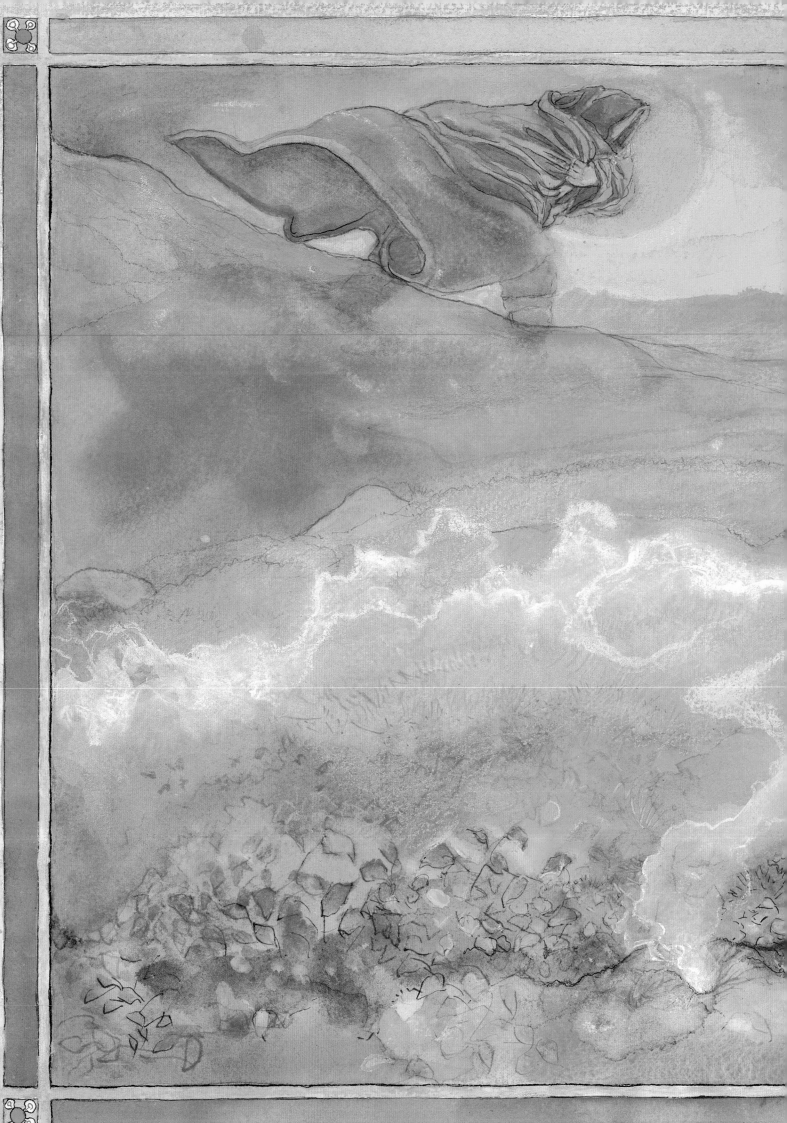

JAMES THURBER

The Great Quillow

ILLUSTRATED BY Steven Kellogg

A TRUMPET CLUB SPECIAL EDITION

Published by The Trumpet Club, Inc.,
a subsidiary of Bantam Doubleday Dell Publishing Group, Inc.,
1540 Broadway, New York, New York 10036.
"A Trumpet Club Special Edition" with the portrayal of a trumpet
and two circles is a registered trademark of
Bantam Doubleday Dell Publishing Group, Inc.

ISBN 0-440-83390-6

This edition published by arrangement with Harcourt Brace & Co., Inc.

Printed in the United States of America
January 1996
10 9 8 7 6 5 4 3 2 1
UPR

The illustrations in this book were done in acrylics,
colored inks, and colored pencils on handmade watercolor paper.
The display type and text type were set in Diotima.
Designed by Camilla Filancia.

To the wonderful Larson family,
with all my love
—S. K.

Once upon a time, in a far country, there lived a giant named Hunder. He was so enormous in height and girth and weight that little waves were set in motion in distant lakes when he walked. His great fingers could wrench a clock from its steeple as easily as a child might remove a peanut from its shell. Every morning he devoured three sheep, a pie made of a thousand apples, and a chocolate as high and as wide as a spinning wheel. It would have taken six ordinary men to lift the great brass key to his front door, and four to carry one of the candles with which he lighted his house.

It was Hunder's way to strip a town of its sheep and apples and chocolate, its leather and cloth, its lumber and tallow and brass, and then move on to a new far village and begin his depredations again. There had been no men strong enough to thwart his evil ways in any of the towns he had set upon and impoverished. He had broken their most formidable weapons between his thumb and forefinger, laughing like the hurricane. And there had been no men cunning enough in any of the towns to bring about his destruction. He had crushed their most ingenious traps with the toe of his mammoth boot, guffawing like a volcano.

One day Hunder strode hundreds and hundreds of leagues and came to a little town in a green valley. It was a staunch little town and a firm little valley, but they quaked with the sound of his coming. The houses were narrow and two stories high; the streets were narrow and cobbled. There were not many people in the town: a hundred men, a hundred women, a hundred children.

Every Tuesday night at seven o'clock a council of ten met to administer the simple affairs of the community. The councillors were the most important tradesmen and artisans of New Moon Street, a short, narrow, cobbled street that ran east and west. These men were the tailor, the butcher, the candymaker, the blacksmith, the baker, the candle-maker, the lamplighter, the cobbler, the carpenter, and the locksmith. After the small business of the tranquil town had been taken care of, the council members sat around and speculated as to the number of stars in the sky, discussed the wonderful transparency of glass, and praised the blueness of violets and the whiteness of snow. Then they made a little fun of Quillow, the toymaker (whose work they considered a rather pretty waste of time), and went home.

Quillow, the toymaker, did not belong to the council but he attended all its meetings. The councilmen were fond of Quillow because of the remarkable toys he made, and because he was a droll and gentle fellow. Quillow made all kinds of familiar playthings on his long and littered workbench: music boxes, jumping jacks, building blocks; but he was famous for a number of little masterpieces of his own invention: a clown who juggled three marbles, a woodman who could actually chop wood, a trumpeter who could play seven notes of a song on a tiny horn, a paperweight in which roses burst into bloom in falling snow.

Quillow was as amusing to look at as any of his toys. He was the shortest man in town, being only five feet tall. His ears were large, his nose was long, his mouth was small, and he had a shock of white hair that stood straight up like a dandelion clock. The lapels of his jacket were wide. He wore a red tie in a deep-pointed collar, and his pantaloons were baggy and unpressed. At Christmas-time each year Quillow made little hearts of gold for the girls of the town and hearts of oak for the boys. He considered himself something of a civic figure, since he had designed the spouting dolphins in the town fountain, the wooden animals on the town merry-go-round, and the twelve scarlet men who emerged from the dial of the town clock on the stroke of every hour and played a melody on little silver bells with little silver hammers.

It was the custom of Quillow's colleagues to shout merrily, "Why, here comes the Great Quillow!" when the toymaker appeared. The lamplighter or the tailor or the locksmith would sometimes creep up behind him and pretend to wind a key in his back as if he were a mechanical figure of his own devising. Quillow took all this in good part, and always, when the imaginary key in his back was turned, he would walk about stiff-legged, with jerky movements of his arms, joining in the fun and increasing the laughter.

It was different on the day the giant arrived. Laughter was hushed and the people hid in their houses and talked in frightened whispers when Hunder's great bulk appeared like a cyclone in the sky and the earth shook beneath him. Panting a little after his thousand-league walk, Hunder pulled up four trees from a hillside to make room for his great hulk and sat down. Hunder surveyed the town and grunted. There was no one to be seen in the streets. Not even a cat crept over the cobblestones.

"Ho, town!" bawled Hunder. The doors shook and the windows rattled. "Ho, town! Send me your clerk that you may hear Hunder's will!"

The town clerk gathered up quill and ink and parchment. "There are ninety-nine other men in town," he grumbled, "but it's the town clerk this, and the town clerk that, and the town clerk everything." He walked out of his house, still grumbling, and trudged across the valley to hear the giant's will.

An hour later the town clerk sat at the head of a long table in the council room and began to call the roll. "We're all here," snapped the blacksmith. "You can see that."

The clerk continued with the roll call. "Baker," he called. "Here," said the baker. "Blacksmith," he droned. "Here," said the blacksmith sourly.

The clerk finished calling the roll and looked over his spectacles. "We have a visitor tonight, as usual," he said, "Quillow, the toymaker. I will make the proper entry in the minutes."

"Never mind the minutes," said the blacksmith. "Read us the demands of Hunder the giant."

The clerk entered Quillow's name in the minutes. "Now," he said, "I will read the minutes of the last meeting."

The candymaker stood up. "Let's dispense with the minutes of the last meeting," he said.

The clerk looked over his spectacles. "It must be properly moved and duly seconded," he said. It was properly moved and duly seconded. "Now read the demands of Hunder the giant!" shouted the blacksmith.

The clerk rapped on the table with his gavel. "Next," he said, "comes unfinished business. We have before us a resolution to regulate the speed of merry-go-rounds."

"Dispense with it!" bawled the blacksmith.

"It must be properly moved and duly seconded," said the clerk. It was properly moved and duly seconded, and the clerk at last unrolled a long scroll of parchment. "We come now," he said, "to the business of the day. I have here the demands of Hunder the giant. The document is most irregular. It does not contain a single 'greeting' or 'whereas' or 'be it known by these presents'!"

Everyone sat motionless as the clerk began to read the scroll. "I, Hunder, must have three sheep every morning," he read.

"That would use up all the sheep in the valley in a week and a fortnight," said the butcher, "and there would be no mutton for our own people."

"I, Hunder, must have a chocolate a day as high and as wide as a spinning wheel," read the town clerk.

"Why, that would exhaust all the chocolate in my storeroom in three days!" cried the candymaker.

The town clerk read from the parchment again. "I, Hunder, must have a new jerkin made for me in a week and a fortnight."

"Why, I would have to work night and day to make a jerkin in a week and a fortnight for so large a giant," gasped the tailor, "and it would use up all the cloth on my shelves and in my basement."

"I, Hunder," went on the town clerk, "must have a new pair of boots within a week and a fortnight."

The cobbler moaned as he heard this. "Why, I would have to work night and day to make a pair of boots for so large a giant in a week and a fortnight," he said. "And it would use up all the leather in my workshop and in my back room."

The council members shook their heads sadly as each demand was read off by the town clerk. Quillow had folded his arms and crossed his legs and shut his eyes. He was thinking, but he looked like a sleeping toy.

"I, Hunder," droned the town clerk, "must have an apple pie each morning made of a thousand apples."

The baker jumped from his chair. "Why, that would use up all the apples and flour and shortening in town in a week and a fortnight," he cried. "And it would take me night and day to make such a pie, so that I could bake no more pies or cakes or cookies, or blueberry muffins or cinnamon buns or cherry boats or strawberry tarts or plum puddings for the people of the town."

All of the councilmen moaned sadly because they loved the list of good things the baker had recited. Quillow still sat with his eyes closed.

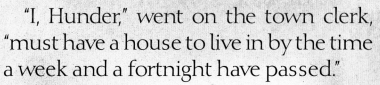

"I, Hunder," went on the town clerk, "must have a house to live in by the time a week and a fortnight have passed."

The carpenter wept openly. "Why, I would have to work night and day to build a house for so large a giant in a week and a fortnight," sobbed the carpenter. "All my nephews and uncles and cousins would have to help me, and it would use up all the wood and pegs and hinges and glass in my shop and in the countryside."

The locksmith stood up and shook his fist in the direction of the hillside on which the giant lay snoring. "I will have to work night and day to make a brass key large enough to fit the keyhole in the front door of the house of so large a giant," he said. "It will use up all the brass in my shop and in the community."

"And I will have to make a candle for his bedside so large it will use up all the wick and tallow in my shop and the world!" said the candlemaker.

"This is the final item," said the town clerk. "I, Hunder, must be told a tale each day to keep me amused."

Quillow opened his eyes and raised his hand. "I will be the teller of tales," he said. "I will keep the giant amused."

The town clerk put away his scroll.

"Does anyone have any idea how to destroy the giant Hunder?" asked the candymaker.

"I could creep up on him in the dark and set fire to him with my lighter," said the lamplighter.

Quillow looked at him. "The fire of your lighter would not harm him any more than a spark struck by a colt shoe in a meadow," said Quillow.

"Quillow is right," said the blacksmith. "But I could build secretly at night an enormous catapult which would cast a gigantic stone and crush Hunder."

Quillow shook his head. "He would catch the stone as a child catches a ball," said Quillow, "and he would cast it back at the town and squash all our houses."

"I could put needles in his suit," said the tailor.

"I could put nails in his boots," said the cobbler.

"I could put oil in his chocolates," said the candymaker.

"I could put stones in his mutton," said the butcher.

"I could put tacks in his pies," said the baker.

"I could put gunpowder in his candles," said the candlemaker.

"I could make the handle of his brass key as sharp as a sword," said the locksmith.

"I could build the roof of his house insecurely so that it would fall on him," said the carpenter.

"The plans you suggest," said Quillow, "would merely annoy Hunder as the gadfly annoys the horse and the flea annoys the dog."

"Perhaps the Great Quillow has a plan of his own," said the blacksmith with a scornful laugh.

"Has the Great Quillow a plan?" asked the candymaker, with a faint sneer.

The little toymaker did not answer. The councillors got up and filed slowly and sadly from the council room. That night none of them wound the imaginary key in Quillow's back.

Quillow did not leave the council chamber for a long time, and when he walked through New Moon Street, all the shops of the councilmen were brightly lighted and noisily busy. There was a great ringing and scraping and thumping and rustling. The blacksmith was helping the locksmith make the great brass key for Hunder's house. The carpenter was sawing and planing enormous boards. The baker was shaping the crust for a gigantic pie, and his wife and apprentice were peeling a thousand apples. The butcher was dressing the first of the three sheep. The tailor was cutting the cloth for Hunder's jerkin. The cobbler was fitting together mammoth pieces of leather for Hunder's boots. The candymaker was piling all his chocolate upon his largest table, while his wife and his daughter made soft filling in great kettles. The candlemaker had begun to build the monumental candle for Hunder's bedside.

As Quillow reached the door of his shop, the town clock in its steeple began to strike, the moon broke out of a patch of cloud, and the toymaker stood with his hand on the door latch to watch the twelve little men in scarlet hats and jackets and pantaloons emerge, each from his own numeral, to make the night melodious with the sound of their silver hammers on the silver bells of the round white dial.

Inside his shop, Quillow lighted the green-shaded lamp over his workbench, which was littered with odds and ends and beginnings and middles of all kinds of toys. Working swiftly with his shining tools, Quillow began to make a figure eight inches high out of wire and cloth and leather and wood. When it was finished it looked like a creature you might come upon hiding behind a tulip or playing with toads. It had round eyes, a round nose and a wide mouth, and no hair. It was blue from head to foot. Its face was blue, its jacket was blue, its pantaloons were blue, and its feet were blue.

As Quillow stood examining the toy, the lamplighter stuck his head in the door without knocking, stared for a moment, and went away. Quillow smiled with satisfaction and began to make another blue man. By the time the first cock crowed he had made ten blue men and put them away in a long wooden chest with a heavy iron clasp.

The lamplighter turned out the last streetlight, the sun rose, the crickets stopped calling, and the clock struck five. Disturbed by the changing pattern of light and sound, the giant on the hillside turned in his sleep. Around a corner into New Moon Street tiptoed the town crier. "Sh!" he said to the lamplighter. "Don't wake the giant."

"Sh!" said the lamplighter. "His food may not be ready."

The town crier stood in the cobbled street and called softly, "Five o'clock, and all's well!"

All the doors in New Moon Street except Quillow's flew open.

"The pie is baked," said the baker.

"The chocolate is made," said the candymaker.

"The sheep are dressed," said the butcher.

"I worked all night on the great brass key," said the locksmith, "and the blacksmith helped me with his hammer and anvil."

"I have scarcely begun the enormous candle," said the candlemaker.

"I am weary of sawing and planing," said the carpenter.

"My fingers are already stiff," said the tailor, "and I have just started the giant's jerkin."

"My eyes are tired," said the cobbler, "and I have hardly begun to make his boots."

The sun shone full on the giant's face, and he woke up and yawned loudly. The councillors jumped, and a hundred children hid in a hundred closets.

"Ho!" roared Hunder. It was the sign the blacksmith had waited for. He drove his wagon drawn by four horses into New Moon Street and climbed down.

"Ho!" roared the giant.

"Heave," grunted the councillors as they lifted the sheep onto the wagon.

"Ho!" roared the giant.

"Heave," grunted the councillors, and up went the pie.

"Ho!" roared the giant.

"Heave," grunted the councillors, and they set the great chocolate in place.

Hunder watched the loading of the wagon, licking his lips and growling like a cave full of bulldogs.

The councillors climbed up on the wagon and the blacksmith yelled "Giddap!" and then "Whoa!" He glared about him. "Where is Quillow?" he demanded. "Where is that foolish little fellow?"

"He was in his shop at midnight," said the lamplighter, "making toys."

The nine other councillors snorted.

"He could have helped with the key," said the locksmith.

"The pie," said the baker.

"The sheep," said the butcher.

"The boots," said the cobbler.

At this, Quillow bounced out of his shop like a bird from a clock, bowing and smiling.

"Well!" snarled the blacksmith.

"Ho!" roared Hunder.

"Good morning," said Quillow. He climbed up on the wagon and the blacksmith spoke to each horse in turn. (Their names were Lobo, Bolo, Olob, and Obol.)

19

"I worked all night with my hammer and anvil," said the blacksmith as the horses lurched ahead, "helping the locksmith with the great brass key." He scowled at Quillow. "The lamplighter tells us *you* spent the night making toys."

"Making toys," said Quillow cheerily, "and thinking up a tale to amuse the giant Hunder."

The blacksmith snorted. "And a hard night you must have spent hammering out your tale."

"And twisting it," said the locksmith.

"And leveling it," said the carpenter.

"And rolling it out," said the baker.

"And stitching it up," said the tailor.

"And fitting it together," said the cobbler.

"And building it around a central thread," said the candlemaker.

"And dressing it up," said the butcher.

"And making it not too bitter and not too sweet," said the candymaker.

When the wagon came to a stop at Hunder's feet, the giant clapped his hands, and Quillow and the councillors were blown to the ground. Hunder roared with laughter and unloaded the wagon in half a trice.

"Tell me your silly names," said Hunder, "and what you do."

The new slaves of Hunder, all except Quillow, bowed in turn and told the giant who they were and what they did. Quillow remained silent.

"You, smallest of men, you with the white hair, who are you?" demanded Hunder.

"I am Quillow, the teller of tales," said the toymaker, but unlike the others he did not bow to the giant.

"Bow!" roared Hunder.

"Wow!" shouted Quillow.

The councillors started back in dismay at the toymaker's impertinence, their widening eyes on Hunder's mighty hands, which closed and then slowly opened. The black scowl cleared from the giant's brow and he laughed suddenly.

"You are a fairly droll fellow," he said. "Perhaps your tales will amuse me. If they do not, I will put you in the palm of my hand and blow you so far it will take men five days to find you. Now be off to your work, the rest of you!"

As the wagon carried the frightened councillors back to town, Quillow sat on the ground and watched the giant eat a sheep as an ordinary man might eat a lark. "Now," said Hunder, "tell me a tale."

"Once upon a time," began Quillow, crossing his legs and tickling a cricket with a blade of grass, "a giant came to our town from a thousand leagues away, stepping over the hills and rivers. He was so mighty a giant that he could stamp upon the ground with his foot and cause the cows in the fields to turn flip-flops in the air and land on their feet again."

"Garf," growled Hunder, "I can stamp upon the ground with my foot and empty a lake of its water."

"I have no doubt of that, O Hunder," said Quillow, "for the thunder is your plaything and the mountains are your stool. But the giant who came over the hills and rivers many and many a year ago was a lesser giant than Hunder. He was weak. He fell ill of a curious malady. He was forced to run to the ocean and bathe in the yellow waters, for only the yellow waters in the middle of the sea could cure the giant."

"Rowf," snarled Hunder, picking up another sheep. "That giant was a goose, that giant was a grasshopper. *Hunder* is never sick." The giant smote his chest and then his stomach mighty blows without flinching, to show how strong he was.

"This other giant," said Quillow, "had no ailment of the chest or the stomach or the mouth or the ears or the eyes or the arms or the legs."

"Where else can a giant have an ailment?" demanded Hunder.

Quillow looked dreamily across the green valley toward the town, which was bright in the sun. "In the mind," said Quillow, "for the mind is a strange and intricate thing. In lesser men than Hunder, it is subject to mysterious maladies."

"Wumf," said the giant, beginning his third sheep. "Hunder's mind is strong like the rock." He smote himself heavily across the forehead without wincing.

"No one to this day knows what brought on this dreadful disease in the mind of the other giant," said Quillow. "Perhaps he killed a turtle after sundown, or ran clockwise thrice around a church in the dark of the moon, or slept too close to a field of asphodel."

Hunder picked up the pie and began to devour it. "Did this goose, this grasshopper, have pains in his head?" he asked. "Look, teller of tales!" Hunder banged his head savagely against a tree, and the trunk of the tree snapped in two. The giant grinned, showing his jagged teeth.

"This other giant," said Quillow, "suffered no pain. His symptoms were marvelous and dismaying. First he heard the word. For fifteen minutes one morning, beginning at a quarter of six, he heard the word."

"Harumph!" said Hunder, finishing his pie and reaching for his chocolate. "What was the word the giant heard for fifteen minutes one day?"

"The word was 'woddly,'" said Quillow. "All words were one word to him. All words were 'woddly.'"

"All words are different to Hunder," said the giant. "And do you call this a tale you have told me? A blithering goose of a giant hears a word and you call that a tale to amuse Hunder?"

Quillow arose as the clock in the steeple struck six and the scarlet figures came out to play the silver bells.

"I hear all words," said Hunder. "This is a good chocolate; otherwise I should put you in the palm of my hand and blow you over the housetops."

"I shall bring you a better tale tomorrow," said Quillow. "Meanwhile, be sure to see the first star over your left shoulder, do not drink facing downstream, and always sleep with your heart to the east."

"Why should Hunder practice this foolish rigmarole?" asked the giant.

"No one knows to this day," said Quillow, "what caused the weird illness in the mind of the other giant." But Hunder gave only a murmurous growl in reply, for he had lain down again on the hillside and closed his eyes. Quillow smiled as he saw that the giant lay with his heart to the east.

The toymaker spent the day making twenty more little blue men and when the first owl hooted he stood in the doorway of his shop and whistled. The hundred children collected in the cobbled street before the toyshop from every nook and corner and cranny and niche of the town. "Go to your homes," said Quillow, "each Sue and John of you, each Nora and Joe, and tell your fathers and mothers to come to the merry-go-round in the carnival grounds one quarter-hour before the moon comes over the hill. Say that Quillow has a plan to destroy the giant Hunder."

The group of children broke like the opening of a rose and the cobbled streets rang with the sound of their running.

Even the scowling blacksmith, the scornful lamplighter, the mumbling town crier, and the fussy town clerk (who had spent the day searching for an ancient treaty the people of the town had once signed with a giant) came at the appointed hour to hear what Quillow had to say.

"What is this clown's whim that brings us here like sheep?" demanded the blacksmith.

Quillow climbed up on the merry-go-round, sat on a swan, and spoke. At first there was a restless stir like wind in the grass, but as Quillow explained his plan, even the chattering wives fell silent. Quillow finished speaking as the moon peeped over the hill, and the hundred men and the hundred women and the hundred children straggled away from the carnival grounds.

"It will never work," said the lamplighter.

"It is worth trying," said the candymaker.

"I have a better plan," said the town crier. "Let all the women and all the children stand in the streets and gaze sorrowfully at the giant, and perhaps he will go away."

His wife took him by the arm and led him home. "We will try Quillow's plan," she said. "He has a magic, the little man."

The next morning, just as the clock in the steeple struck five, the weary blacksmith, with Quillow sitting beside him, drove the wagon loaded with three sheep and a fresh apple pie and another monster chocolate to where the giant sat on the hillside. Hunder unloaded the wagon in a third of a trice, placed the food beside him on the hill, and began to gnaw at a sheep. "Tell me a tale, smallest of men," he said, "and see to it that I do not nod, or I shall put you in the palm of my hand and blow you through yonder cloud."

"Once upon a time," began Quillow, "there was a king named Anderblusdaferafan, and he had three sons named Ufabrodoborobe, Quamdelrodolanderay, and Tristolcomofarasee."

"Those names are hard names," said Hunder. "Tell me those names again that I may remember them." So Quillow started over slowly with "Once upon a time," and again the giant made him repeat the names.

"Why did this king and his sons have such long and difficult names?" demanded Hunder, eating his second sheep.

"Ah," said Quillow, "it was because of the king's mother, whose name was Isoldasadelofandaloo."

"Tell me her name once more," said Hunder, "that I may remember it." So Quillow told him the name again slowly.

Thus the wily Quillow, who really had thought of no tale to tell, wasted the long minutes as the hands of the clock in the steeple crept around the dial. As they neared a quarter of six o'clock, Quillow went on. "One day as the king and his sons were riding through the magical forest," he said, "they came upon a woddly. Woddly woddly woddly. Woddly woddly woddly."

The giant's eyes grew narrow, then wide.

"Woddly woddly woddly," said Quillow, "woddly woddly woddly woddly."

The giant dropped the chocolate he was eating. "Say it with words!" he bellowed. "You say naught but 'woddly.'"

Quillow looked surprised. "Woddly woddly woddly woddly woddly woddly woddly woddly," he said. "Woddly woddly woddly."

"Can this be the malady come upon me?" cried the giant. He caught the toymaker up in his hand. "Or do you seek to frighten Hunder?" he roared.

"Woddly woddly woddly," said Quillow, trembling in spite of himself, as he pointed to a farmer in a field and to a child gathering cowslips and to the town crier making his rounds. "Woddly woddly woddly," repeated Quillow.

The giant dropped Quillow and arose. He strode to where the farmer stood and picked him up. "Say words!" bawled Hunder. "Say many words!"

"Woddly," said the farmer, and Hunder dropped him in the field and turned to the child.

"What is your name?" roared Hunder.

"Woddly woddly," said the child.

Hunder stepped over to the town crier. "What is the time of day?" he bellowed.

"Woddly woddly," said the town crier.

Then Hunder shouted questions at men and women and children who came running into the streets. He asked them how old they were, and what day it was, and where they were going, and how they were feeling. And they said "Woddly" and "Woddly woddly" and "Woddly woddly woddly."

Hunder strode back across the green valley to where Quillow sat brushing flies off the half-eaten chocolate. "It is the malady! I have heard the word! It is the malady!" cried Hunder. "What am I to do to cure the malady?"

Just then the clock in the steeple struck six, and as the scarlet men came out to play the bells, Quillow spoke reproachfully. "I was telling you how the king and his three sons rode through the magical forest," he said, "when you picked me up and flung me to the earth and ran away, leaving your chocolate uneaten."

The giant sat on the ground, panting heavily, his lower teeth showing. "I heard the word," he said. "All men said the word."

"What word?" asked Quillow.

"Woddly," said the giant.

"That is but the first symptom," said Quillow reassuringly, "and it has passed. Look at the chimneys of the town. Are they not red?"

Hunder looked. "Yes, the chimneys are red," said Hunder. "Why do you ask if the chimneys are red?"

"So long as the chimneys are red," said Quillow, "you have no need to worry, for when the second symptom is upon you, the chimneys of the town turn black."

"I see only red chimneys," said the giant. "But what could have caused Hunder to hear the word?" he asked as he hurled the half-eaten chocolate far away over the roofs of the town.

"Perhaps," said Quillow, "you stepped on a centaur's grave or waked the sleeping unicorn or whistled on Saint Nillin's Day."

Hunder the giant rested badly on the hillside that night, twisting and turning in his sleep, tormented by ominous dreams. While he slept, the youngest and most agile men of the town, in black smocks and slippered feet, climbed to the roofs of the houses and shops, each carrying a full pail and a brush, and painted all the chimneys black.

Quillow, the toymaker, worked busily all night, and by the dark hour before the dawn, had made twenty more blue men so that he now had fifty blue men in all. He put the new ones with the others he had made, in the large chest with the iron clasp.

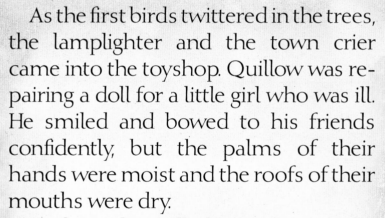

As the first birds twittered in the trees, the lamplighter and the town crier came into the toyshop. Quillow was repairing a doll for a little girl who was ill. He smiled and bowed to his friends confidently, but the palms of their hands were moist and the roofs of their mouths were dry.

"Perhaps he will detect your trick," said the lamplighter.

"Perhaps he will smash all our houses," said the town crier.

As the three men talked, they heard the giant stirring on the hillside. He rubbed his eyes with his great knuckles, yawned with the sound of a sinking ship, and stretched his powerful arms. The toymaker and the lamplighter and the town crier watched through a window and held their breath.

Hunder sat up, staring at the ground and running his fingers through his hair. Then slowly he lifted his head and looked at the town. He closed his eyes tightly and opened them again and stared. His mouth dropped open and he lurched to his feet. "The chimneys!" he bellowed. "The chimneys are black! The malady is upon me again!"

Quillow began to scamper through the cobbled streets and across the green valley as the giant's eyes rolled and his knees trembled. "Teller of tales, smallest of men!" bellowed Hunder. "Tell me what I must do. The chimneys are black!" Quillow reached the feet of the giant, panting and flushed. "Look, teller of tales," said the giant, "name me fairly the color of yonder chimneys."

Quillow turned and looked toward the town. "The chimneys are red, O Hunder," he said. "The chimneys are red. See how they outdo the red rays of the sun."

"The rays of the sun are red," said Hunder, "but the chimneys of the town are black."

"You tremble," said Quillow, "and your tongue hangs out, and these are indeed the signs of the second symptom. But still there is no real danger, for you do not see the blue men. Or do you see the blue men, O Hunder?" he asked.

"I see the men of the town standing in the streets and staring at me," said Hunder. "But their faces are white and they wear clothes of many colors. Why do you ask me if I see blue men?"

Quillow put on a look of grave concern. "When you see the blue men," he said, "it is the third and last symptom of the malady. If that should happen, you must rush to the sea and bathe in the yellow waters or your strength will become the strength of a kitten." The giant groaned. "Perhaps if you fast for a day and a night," said Quillow, "the peril will pass."

"I will do as you say, teller of tales," said the giant, "for you are wise beyond the manner of men. Bring me no food today, tell me no tale." And with a moan Hunder sat back upon the hillside and covered his eyes with his hands.

When Quillow returned to the town, the people cheered him softly and the children flung flowers at his feet. But the blacksmith was skeptical. "The giant is still there on the hillside," he said. "I shall save my cheers and my flowers until the day he is gone, if that day shall ever come." And he stalked back to his smithy to help the locksmith make the great brass key for Hunder's front door.

That noon there was enough mutton and pie and chocolate for all the people of the town, and they ate merrily and well.

Hunder the giant fretted and worried so profoundly during the day that he fell quickly to sleep as the night came. It was a night without moon or stars, as Quillow had hoped. A town owl who lived on the roof of the tavern—at the Sign of the Clock and Soldier—was surprised at the soft and shadowy activities of the toymaker. The bat and the firefly hovered about him in wonder as he worked secretly and swiftly in the green valley at the feet of the snoring giant.

The squirrel and the nightingale watched like figures in a tapestry as he dug and planted in the woods at the giant's head. If the giant thrashed suddenly in his sleep or groaned, the cricket and the frog fell silent in high anxiety. When Quillow's work was finished and he returned to his shop, the bat and the firefly moved in dreamy circles, the squirrel and the nightingale stirred freely again, and the cricket and the frog began to sing. The owl on the roof of the Clock and Soldier nodded and slept. Quillow lay down on his workbench and closed his eyes.

When the scarlet men played the bells of five o'clock, and the first birds twittered in the trees and the gray light came, Quillow awoke and opened his door. The town crier stood in the cobbled street in front of the shop. "Cry the hour," said Quillow. "Cry all's well."

"Five o'clock!" cried the town crier. "Five o'clock and all's well!"

The people crept out of their houses and on the hillside across the green valley, Hunder the giant stirred and yawned and stretched and rubbed his eyes and sat up. He saw that the chimneys were still black, but he grinned at them and winked. "The malady passes," said Hunder. "I see men with white faces wearing clothes of many colors, but I see no blue men." He flexed the muscles of his powerful arms and he smote himself mighty blows upon his brow and chest and stomach. "Ho, councillors!" roared Hunder. "Bring me my sheep and my pie and my chocolate, for I have a vast hunger."

The people fled from the streets, and behind the barred doors and shuttered windows of their houses they listened and trembled. The baker, the butcher, and the candymaker hid under their beds. They had prepared no meal for the giant and they were afraid for their lives. But the brave little toymaker, his white hair flowing like the dandelion clock in the morning wind, ran through the cobbled streets and across the green valley and stood at the giant's feet.

"Behold, I am still a whole man!" bellowed the giant, thumping his brow. "I have heard the word and I have seen the black chimneys, but I have not beheld the blue men."

"That is well," said Quillow, "for he who beholds the blue men must bathe in the yellow waters in the middle of the sea, or else he will dwindle, first to the height of the pussy willow, then to the height of the daffodil, then to the height of the violet, until finally he becomes a small voice in the grass, lost in the thundering of the crickets."

"But I shall remain stronger than the rock and taller than the oak," said Hunder, and he clapped his hands together.

"If you are stronger than the rock and taller than the oak," said Quillow, "then stamp on the ground and make yonder cow in the field turn a flip-flop."

Hunder stood up and chortled with glee. "Behold, smallest of men," he said, "I will make the cow turn twice in the air." He brought his right foot down upon the earth sharply and heavily. The cow turned a double flip-flop in the field, Quillow bounced as high as the giant's belt, and great boughs fell from trees.

But the giant had no eyes for these familiar wonders. He stared at something new under the sun, new and small and terrible. The blue men had come. The blue men were popping high into the air. They popped up in the valley and they popped up in the woods. They popped up from behind stones and they popped up from behind cowslips. They popped up in front of Hunder and they popped up behind him and under him and all around him.

"The blue men!" cried Hunder. "The blue men have come! The world is filled with little blue men!"

"I see no blue men," said Quillow, "but you have begun to shrink like the brook in dry weather, and that is the sign of the third symptom."

"The sea! The sea! Point me to the sea!" bellowed Hunder, who now stood shivering and shaking.

"It is many leagues to the east," said Quillow. "Run quickly toward the rising sun and bathe in the yellow waters in the middle of the sea."

Hunder the giant ran toward the rising sun, and the town trembled as he ran. Pictures fell from walls and plates from plate rails and bricks from chimneys. The birds flew and the rabbits scampered. The cows turned flip-flops in the fields and the brook jumped out of its bed.

A fortnight later a traveler from afar, stopping at the Sign of the Clock and Soldier, told the innkeeper a marvelous tale of how a giant, panting and moaning like a forest on fire, had stumbled down out of the mountains and plunged into the sea, flailing and threshing, and babbling of yellow waters and black chimneys and little blue men; and of how he had floundered farther and farther out to sea until at last he sank beneath the waves, starting a mighty tide rolling to the shore and sending up water spouts as high as the heavens. Then the giant was seen no more, and the troubled waters quieted as the sea resumed its inscrutable cycle of tides under the sun and the moon.

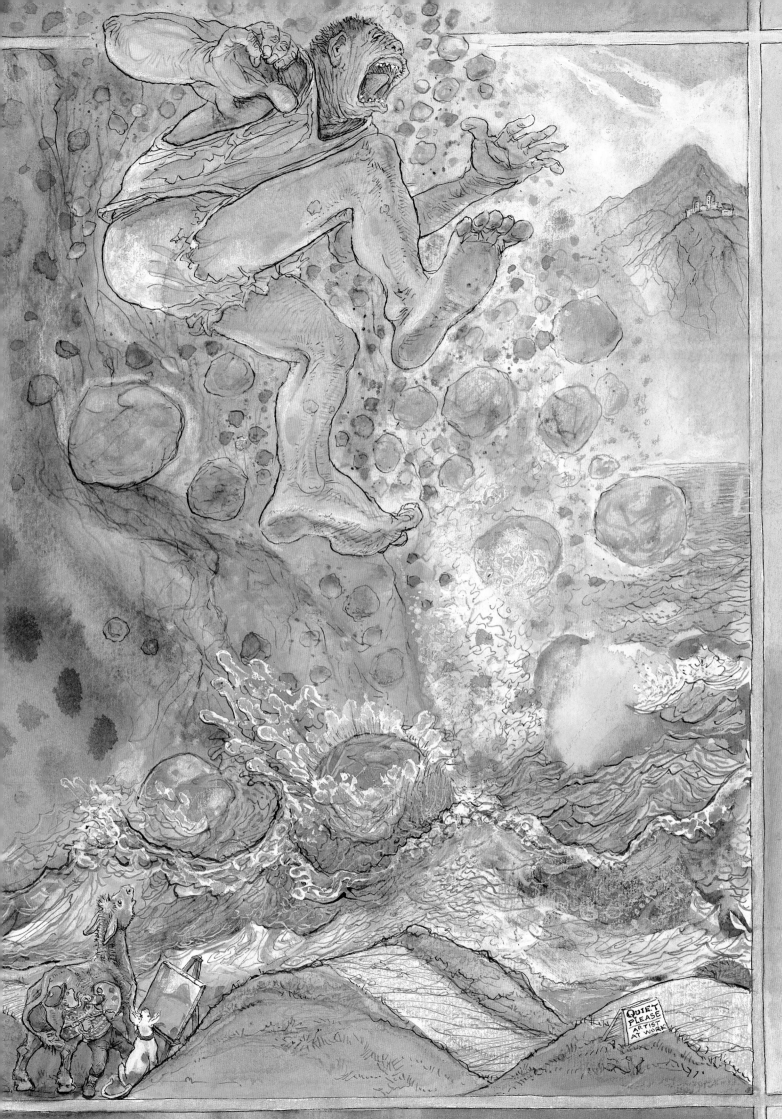

The innkeeper told this tale to the blacksmith, and the blacksmith told it to the locksmith, and the locksmith told it to the baker, and the baker told it to the butcher, and the butcher told it to the tailor, and the tailor told it to the cobbler, and the cobbler told it to the candymaker, and the candymaker told it to the candlemaker, and the candlemaker told it to the town crier, and the town crier told it to the lamplighter, and the lamplighter told it to the toymaker.

As the lamplighter spoke, Quillow put the finishing touches on a new toy, whistling softly, his eyes sparkling. The lamplighter saw that the toy was a tiny replica of Quillow himself.

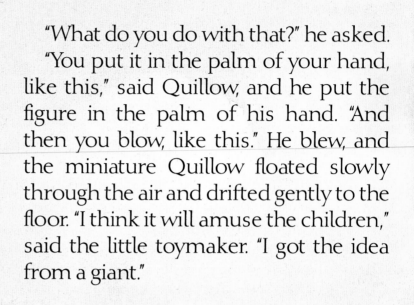

"What do you do with that?" he asked.

"You put it in the palm of your hand, like this," said Quillow, and he put the figure in the palm of his hand. "And then you blow, like this." He blew, and the miniature Quillow floated slowly through the air and drifted gently to the floor. "I think it will amuse the children," said the little toymaker. "I got the idea from a giant."